AF596579

Sweetest

Sins

By

Jessie Knight

This is a work of fiction, intended for adults 18 and over. All characters are 18 and over. Any similarity to real events, people or places is a coincidence.

Published by Jessie Knight, ©2022. All Rights Reserved.

Chapter 1

Nighttime, University Campus 1940's

I walk at a brisk pace, heels clacking against the marbled floor, to the office of my professor of Egyptian studies. The floor to ceiling windows reflect me, walking against the blackness of the night beyond. It's not my first meeting with my professor and my heart beats faster, as I consider what's about to happen.

I made a deal with him, and I don't care that I did. My goal is to graduate at the top of my class and receive my doctorate and if I need to screw my professor, so be it. He's a handsome man, virile, strong, magnetic personality, so in that regard I feel satisfied.

I walk into the classroom lab and head back to his office. My heart beats even faster. I've decided that this relationship will be on my terms. No discussing previous relationships, and no talk of a relationship. Success is what I want, and success is what I shall have.

I rap out a light tap on his door, but Dr. Heimdahl opens it before I can knock.

"Miss Hundine." He waves me into his office.

For a moment it feels like my heart stops as I stare into his big blue eyes. He's dressed in a suit and the cologne that hangs about him is fashionable and pleasant.

"You may hang your coat over there."

I unbutton my overcoat slowly, until the task is finished, and then I push it off my shoulders. He takes a seat and watches me. I slide it off and place it over a chair and turn back to him.

A sense of excitement takes over me, my pulse racing. All I'm wearing is my garter belt and hosiery.

He continues to stare, but moves towards me, flinging off his jacket and shirt as he does so.

"Exquisite. Now lie down on the cot, and spread your thighs for me, Miss Hundine."

I do as I'm told, the cool air in the room hitting my nether region.

"Spread your thighs wider." He commands, his voice deep.

He comes towards me, unzipping his pants as he does so. He drops his ensemble over a chair and his cock springs out, large and unwieldy.

He sits between my legs and moves his fingers up my thighs. Nerves jump in my legs, but I remain still. He watches my reaction, and moves his fingers until he is at the very top of my thighs, and then his fingers begin to stroke the lips that guard the entrance to the tight space inside me.

"Swollen and wet already, Miss Hundine. This arrangement excites you as much as it does me. Tell me something. How hard do you want me to fuck you?"

"Hard, Sir."

"Do you want me to be forceful, Miss Hundine?"

My breathing gets heavier. I like it when he is aggressive.

"Speak."

"Yes, Sir. But, don't forget the condom."

He pulls out a tube from his pants pocket, opens it and glides it over his cock. "Worried about being up the pole, Miss Hundine?"

"You're too cavalier about it."

He laughs. "Forced to bear my child and be my wife. Think of that as I fuck you, Miss Hundine."

I can tell that the idea of it excites him, as he grabs my wrists and holds my arms above my head, mounting me, his body long and firm against mine. He pushes his long, heavy cock into the tight space between my thighs. The pressure increases as he slides it all the way in, and then he commences a stroking motion. In and out, carefully, and slowly. He wants to make this last, and he likes me to struggle against him. He told me on our first meeting that he wanted me to fight him. As if I could match his strength, but I try too anyway.

The cot beneath us creaks with regularity, the only sounds in the still room beside his body slapping into mine, and the sound of panting. I question my reasoning for letting this man push his cock inside me. The strokes get quicker, and he grunts and uses more force. I grimace and let out a sound that is a cross between a moan and a grunt.

He stops, his swollen peter poised at the maximum depth inside my hole. I'm full of him, and uncomfortable. I wasn't going to let him turn me on, but his cunningness and power command a certain respect from me. That and hatred. At least I won't be getting a disease from him. I insisted on a condom. He didn't want to use one, and he laughed at me when I told him that was part of the deal. He said he would think it hilarious if he made me have his baby.

I look up at him, afraid of what I'll see. He stares down at me, an unpleasant smile on his face.

"Remember our deal. You just broke it. You do not hide the fact that you scorn me." He revels in his power over me. He continues to wait, making me feel his displeasure, making me feel fear that I will lose everything I have worked so hard for. I can't let this man get in the way of what I want. I want to be a powerhouse in a man's world, and I won't let him stop me.

“I’m going to finish my pleasure with you Miss Hundine, but I will not pass you because you showed displeasure towards me. Now, if you want your grades, I will have you whenever I call, and in whatever position I wish you to be.”

He gives me a long, hard stare and then commences a few stiff strokes of his penis inside me, as he waits for me to answer him.

“I need your answer now. Remember, you broke the deal.”

“You can’t just have me whenever you want, I have things I have to take care of.”

He pulls out until only the tip of his penis remains at the entry of my slit. I think he is going to pull out and then I will have to face the magistrate and be deported and my grade will be an ‘F’. I have come too far to let this go. My legs are already spread. Besides if he’s fucking me, he’s probably fucking other young grad students from other departments, so how much can he really want me? It’s just a power trip, that’s all it is.

“It’s whenever I want you and wherever I want you.”

It can’t be much worse than this, the room off the lab, the room where someone, probably him, placed a creaky cot. I’m sure it’s not for sleeping but for fucking. How many others has he had beneath him like me?

Reluctantly, I give him his answer. “Okay.”

“Place a smile on your lips Miss Hundine and moan for me like the little slut that you are.”

I give a grimace of a smile up at him, the cock that he is. Total cock. Big dick, dripping with lust.

“Better. Now moan like your life depends on it because it does.”

I moan, softly. I am afraid that someone will come into the lab while he is fucking me, and I don't want that. I don't want anyone to know how desperate I am to get to the top in a man's world.

"Louder Miss Hundine. Louder. That's it. I knew you could do better."

The cot creaks furiously as he drives his penis between my thighs. My bottom is wet and sweaty and swollen from the friction of his body slapping against mine. His strokes are long and hard and forceful. I sense that his rocket is about to shoot its payload of cum.

I grip the sides of the cot, trying to quell the banging noises he is making.

"Please, someone could be in there." I whisper to him.

"Miss Hundine, do you think I really give a fuck who's in there? Do you really think for one second that anyone cares that the tenured Professor of Egyptian Studies is fucking a grad student?"

It shuts me up. He was right, probably not. To my horror, I hear the sound of knocking on the door adjoining the lab.

"Dr. Heimdahl. Are you there?"

I recognize my fellow grad student, Peter Russell. He is British, serious, always with his nose to the grindstone. And good looking, not that I care much. I'm not looking for a long term boyfriend. But, this blows. I freeze underneath Dr. Heimdahl.

"Clearly, I am busy Mr. Russell. Don't bother me again."

Dr. Heimdahl recommences his stroking motion, his penis so engorged that I can tell it's about to explode.

I whisper harshly. "He can hear."

“Let him hear it. He’s not a boy. That will teach him to come to the lab at eleven in the evening.”

I tense my body. The professor continues to fuck me with intensity and without care about the amount of noise the cot makes, as it creaks and bangs, until at last, he cums with a tremendous shuddering push, with such force that it makes me cry out.

My clit and vagi lips are swollen and wanting. Mr. Russell is in the next room and the professor looks at me expectantly. I want to feel my own release, but I decide to wait until I am in the privacy of my own quarters. Even though women have been able to vote for 20 some years, it’s not considered acceptable to talk about an act that has kept the human population growing for thousands of years. Let alone have sex with someone you’re not married to.

Dr. Heimdahl throws the used condom into a wastepaper basket and pulls on his trousers. I look up at him, feeling dread at facing Mr. Russell. I hastily pull on my silk stockings. When I am finished dressing, and turning to leave, Dr. Heimdahl walks behind me and runs his hand over my silken thigh. His hand is firm and large and continues its glide up my leg until it cups my bottom. He squeezes my backside. “Remember Miss Hundine, whenever and wherever.”

The scent of his aftershave fills my nostrils as he presses in behind me and runs his other hand over my lower belly and up my torso until it comes to my tit. He cups my tit in his hand and gently squeezes. He whispers in my ear, “It will be soon.”

He opens the door to the lab, once we have dressed, and winks at Mr. Russell. “I was just giving Miss Hundine a lesson in hidden archaeology.” Dr. Heimdahl laughs and pats my bottom firmly, as he looks directly at Mr. Russell. A blush shoots through my body from the top of my head to my feet. Mr. Russell looks at me and then looks away quickly. He knows. I tilt my head downwards and make a dash for the door.

“Wait, Miss Hundine. I will escort you home. It’s not safe for a woman to be alone here. Don’t you agree Mr. Russell?”

“Yes, Dr. Heimdahl.”

I take it for what it is, an excuse to find out where I live, so that he can have access to my body whenever and wherever he wants. And now I know how bad it’s going to be. This isn’t going to be some simple offing. I am in a world of trouble, and I don’t know how I’m going to get out of it.

Chapter 2

My roommate is gone, and I have time to work on my paper. I sit at the table and type, trying not to think about the deal that I have struck. Dr. Heimdahl said he might stop by at any time, and that I had to drop whatever I was doing and spread my legs for him. If he wasn't the most brilliant man in his field, I never would have given the bargain a second thought. But I want to learn from the best mind. And Dr. Heimdahl? What does he want? He wants access to my body. So far he hasn't gone overboard. But then the phone rings, and I jump.

I pick up the black handle, put it to my ear and wind the curly cord around my finger. My pulse starts to race.

"Miss Hundine. It's Mrs. Marshland."

Dr. Heimdahl's secretary. We exchange pleasant greetings. I don't think she knows about my deal with Dr. Heimdahl. This woman is very religious, and I don't think she would ever consider sex outside of matrimony. It's something that good girls in our society don't do.

"Dr. Heimdahl needs to speak with you."

"Okay."

"He wants you to come into his office. It's about the upcoming trip to Cairo."

"I see."

"He needs you to come in right away."

"Yes. Mrs. Marshland. I understand."

I gather my jacket and my heart skips a beat. I don't know why, but this deal excites me on some level. Excites and repulses me.

There's a knock at the door, and I peek out. It's him. I open it, my heart pounding. I knew he would come to my apartment at some point.

"Miss Hundine. Are you going to allow me entrance?"

I stare at him for a moment, and then I let him in, as I take a cautious glance around. I don't see anyone and that gives me a brief sense of relief. I lock the door and take his overcoat.

"My roommate could be back at any minute."

He ignores my comment. "Bare your breasts for me, Miss Hundine."

His commands get me excited on some level, and I obey him. I slide my sweater over my head, unhook my brazier from behind, and drop it to the chair.

He doesn't touch me, but stares at my tits, and I observe that the front of his pants is filled with a massive bulge. His penis is spectacularly large, and I know he is salivating inside.

"Beg me to fill you up."

"Please Dr. Heimdahl. Fill me up."

"Do better than that. Convince me."

I gather my sweater and brazier and cock my finger at him, motioning him to follow me into my bedroom.

He follows me in.

"Give me your scarf." He commands.

I hand it to him.

"Undress."

I follow his instructions and take all of my clothes off, my nipples erect as I stand naked before him.

"Lie down on your bed."

I lie down, watching as he releases his belt and lets his pants and shirt fall to the floor. As soon as his body is naked, I cannot help but notice the massive erection his trousers have been concealing. His penis points skyward, thick and full. He walks to me and takes my hands and binds them with my scarf to the brass post of my headboard.

"Suck." He lets his cock dangle in front of my face, and I take it in my mouth as he ties my hands to the post.

I gag as his member fills the entirety of my mouth and hits the back of my throat. He slightly withdraws and then thrusts again.

"Miss Hundine. What do you want me to do with you?"

"Dr. Heimdahl. Fuck me." My words are garbled, since my mouth is filled with him.

"Beg."

"Please fuck me."

"Convince me that you need to be fucked."

"I can't reach my pussy. I need you to stroke it for me. Please."

He crouches over me on the single mattress and reverses positions so that his mouth is between my thighs and my mouth stays full of him.

"Bare and smooth, you shaved it for me." He sounds pleased. His tongue begins to slide along my pussy lips causing an aching sensation to build between my thighs.

"Oh. Oh. Oh."

His tongue finds my clit and makes firm strokes against the organ until the pressure builds to almost bursting. When I can't stand it anymore, he stops and moves his mouth to my breasts and sucks on each tit.

I didn't want this bargain, but now my resistance to him is eroding. He makes my body hum.

"Please. Oh. Please."

"What do you want Miss Hundine?"

"I need your cock inside me. Now. But, use a condom." My voice is like a growl.

He grumbles, but slowly removes his organ from me and makes a grab for the pocket of his trousers. He pulls out a slim box of redi-wet rubbers, opens a tube and proceeds to cloak himself. I breathe a sigh of relief.

I'm determined that I will go to Egypt with his team, and I can't get pregnant. I've tried to be very cautious, despite the situation I find myself in.

"Demanding little slut, aren't you?" He says with a smile on his face as he mounts me in a proper missionary position. There is indescribable pleasure inside me as he pushes his cock into me. It's heavy and full. And when he begins to slide himself in and out of me, my body takes over. My hips thrust into his.

The bed springs creak and protest with the motions of his thrusts and mine. His cock ramming inside me with great force.

"I like having you tied to this bed, Miss Hundine, my very own sex slave. Tell me you like it."

"You talk too much."

"You've got a pert mouth Miss Hundine." He grips my tied-up wrists and eases himself inside me, proceeding to stroke me, in and out, each thrust harder, until my single bed, with its metal headboard, begins to bump the wall in rhythm. I'm pretty sure it's going to mark the wall, but he doesn't seem to care.

"Is this better, Miss Hundine? More thrusting, less conversation?"

The bed springs creak in protest.

He continues to thrust himself inside me, until he is at the verge of his climax.

The door to my apartment opens, and laughter fills the kitchen. My roommate, and a friend. My eyes go wide.

"Shut the door." I whisper harshly.

My professor laughs, pulls out of me, saunters to the door, and slams it shut.

"Margie?" Jane calls.

I close my eyes and bite my lip. My professor laughs in my ear and continues to stroke me, bed springs creaking, headboard slamming and all. He climaxes with a mighty crescendo, finishing by collapsing on me, breathing soundly.

The sensitive area, between my thighs, throbs, begging for a release.

Professor Heimdahl laughs, pulls out, and discards the used condom in the trash.

Jane knocks on the door. "Are you all right in there, Margie?"

"I'm fine, a little headache. I just need to rest."

"I'll bring you an ice pack and an aspirin."

"No. No. I'll be out. Don't worry about me."

"Ok. If you say so."

Her footsteps recede and I release a sigh and question my choices. I've really done a number on myself. Why did I choose this? Is it really getting me what I wanted? I wanted to be powerful in a man's world, but there are so many pitfalls.

Something about this arrangement charges me up, though, and gets me off.

A boldness takes over me. If I'm going to commit to this ridiculous arrangement, I might as well enjoy it.

"Untie me."

Dr. Heimdahl unties me, and I sit up and reach under my bed for my scalp massager. I have discovered a way to experience the most delightful sensations ever felt.

He watches in amusement as I plug it in and turn it on.

"Good for a headache, Miss Hundine?"

"It has other uses as well. Women climax. I have discovered that I can experience multiples with this. And by my own hand, though this makes it easier."

"I want to see this."

I turn over. "Push a finger inside me, maybe two."

He complies with my request and despite my best efforts, I thump the bed as nearly as hard as he did to get myself off. Spiraling sensations build inside me as the throbbing intensifies, until, I burst in ecstasy, as wild electrical impulses charge though the space between my legs and my pussy clamps down on Dr. Heimdahl's fingers.

"Ummm. Oh. Yes." I glide over the massager and his fingers until the sensations subside.

He pulls out his fingers, staring at me with an expression of awe.

"I want another."

"You want to do this again?"

My face heats and I nod.

It doesn't take me very long to experience another, just as good. So good, that my toes curl in ecstasy.

I flip over and face him, sweaty and red faced, but happy.

He leans towards me, and takes my cheeks in his hands, his long fingers gently stroking the sides of my face as his eyes search mine. After a long moment of staring at each other, he leans to me and kisses me on the lips.

It surprises me. We’ve never touched lips before.

Chapter 3

I watch discreetly, as the woman I'm fucking strides across the lawn, a swing in her step. Her honey blond hair lies in graceful curls around her pretty oval face, her full bosom bouncing with every step. My cock is aroused as I watch, and I start to think of how and where our next encounter is going to occur. There's a little smile on her pouty lips, and I like to think that maybe it is because she is on the way to my classroom, and on the way to see me.

A group of male grad students walks behind her, and I continue to observe as Mr. Russell, one of the leaders of the group, and one of my brightest students makes an obscene gesture in the direction of Miss Hundine.

I've never known myself to be a particularly rageful person before, but something foreign, I suppose I must call it rage because it is the closest thing I can call it, arises within me. *Am I becoming a protective of Miss Hundine?*

No. I want her to fuck. That was our bargain. That is all. Besides, she made it very clear to me that she didn't want a relationship. Just fucking and good grades. Sometimes I wonder if she really believes I would fail her. Truth is, I wouldn't, she's just as intelligent as any of my male students. But it hasn't hurt me for her to believe it because I enjoy her in the sack immensely.

Mr. Russell leaves the group and begins to walk beside her. The audacity. We'll see about this.

Miss Hundine enters the classroom first, followed by Mr. Russell. Mr. Russell puts a hand on her bottom and Miss Hundine swirls, face red, and slaps him across the face.

Mr. Russell blushes, an angry look on his face.

"You're only here because you're with the professor. He scores you higher than anyone else, and we all know why."

"It doesn't give you the right to touch me. Don't you ever touch me again."

"You let him touch you."

I close my fist, approach him, and swing hard. Mr. Russell whirls backwards upon contact with my fist and hits the door.

"Don't ever return to my classroom." I spit out, feeling revulsion fill me.

Everyone stares.

"She's not here because of her intelligence." Mr. Russell bursts out, gaining his balance and striding towards me. He looks murderous, like he wants to strike me. "Everyone knows you're fucking her."

Unfortunately for him, I'm bigger, and I trained as a boxer during my days as an undergrad. It paid the bills.

He closes his fist and takes a swing at me. I curl my fist again and give him a swift undercut to the jaw. He wheels backwards and falls to the floor.

I tense, waiting for him to get up.

He stands, slightly unsteadily, as the class looks on.

"Get out of my classroom."

Mr. Russell points at me, and yells, his tone venomous. "You will be in trouble for this. Mark my words."

"Come on." One of his sidekick's mutters. "Leave, you're embarrassing yourself."

"Apologize to Miss Hundine."

"She deserves everything she gets. She's a dime a dozen whore."

“Miss Hundine clearly has more common sense and intelligence than you Mr. Russell. Her grades were won, fair and square, without help from me. But, I will not allow you to call her baseless names.”

My fist curls again and I land a blow to his cheek, knocking him to the floor. He seems to come to his senses, turns and stumbles out the door.

Miss Hundine stands, face red, fanning herself with her notepad. Sweat beads at the edges of her hairline.

“Class dismissed. There are matters I need to attend to regarding this incident.”

I look at the men gathered around, waiting for my instruction. “Are there any here who witnessed the treatment of Miss Hundine by Mr. Russell?”

I gather the names and we head to Old Main to make a report. I’ve no doubt that Mr. Russell will tell his father and since his father is a leading source of endowments to the university, there will need to be i’s dotted and t’s crossed.

Chapter 4

The process takes weeks, but I keep my job. Miss Hundine and I continue to see each other on the sly. The semester is nearly over, and I find that she is in my thoughts nearly all the time. She will receive her doctorate and be done with me. Yet, I find, I cannot be done with her.

We used each other and got what we wanted in the bargain. But now that our time is ending, I am finding myself sentimental. *Odd for a person like me.*

One day I find myself at a travel agency and the next, at a jewelry shop. I tell myself that she won't want to marry an old fool like me. She was using me. She is young and beautiful. She will move on, maybe marry someone rich.

However, once I've gotten it in my head that I will accomplish a task, I rarely back down. Perhaps it is due to one too many blows to the head back in my boxing days.

I pick out a ring. A very special ring. A sapphire surrounded by diamond petals, to match the brilliant deep sapphire blue of her eyes. *I am getting sentimental.*

I buy two complete ticket packages bound for Egypt, one for me and one for her. If she refuses my offer, I will go alone. But somewhere deep inside me, I know that if she refuses, I will not enjoy going without her.

I plan on taking her in public to Dilly's, a popular restaurant nearby, and there, I will pop the question. But before I do, I want to rendezvous with her in my car at our Lovers Lane.

Chapter 5

Professor Heimdahl picks me up, and we drive to Lover's Lane in his convertible. I'm due to graduate in 3 weeks and the weather is a balmy 70 degrees. The cherry trees are in bloom, and he steps out and walks to my side of the car.

For some reason, he seems tense, and not himself. Perhaps because our bargain is coming to an end. I'm not sure. All I know is that the sexual bond we've developed in the past year is incredible and now that it may be ending, I'm starting to feel sad. I wasn't expecting this.

It's very romantic here, and we stroll down the pathway, not holding hands, because we can't show any affection in public.

"It's very beautiful here."

"It is." He looks down the path and then at me. He swallows hard, his jaw clenching.

We walk a little further and come to a beautiful overlook with a view of the river.

"Do you want to stop for a moment?"

He nods. I look out at the view, breathe in the scent of fresh earth and springtime, and watch him as he paces. He stops as a couple walks by, hand in hand. After they pass, he resumes his pacing.

"Professor Heimdahl. Whatever is the matter?"

He turns to me, stares into my eyes, and just like that, everything slows down around us.

"Miss Hundine." He walks towards me.

I keep my eyes on him, unsure of what he is about to do.

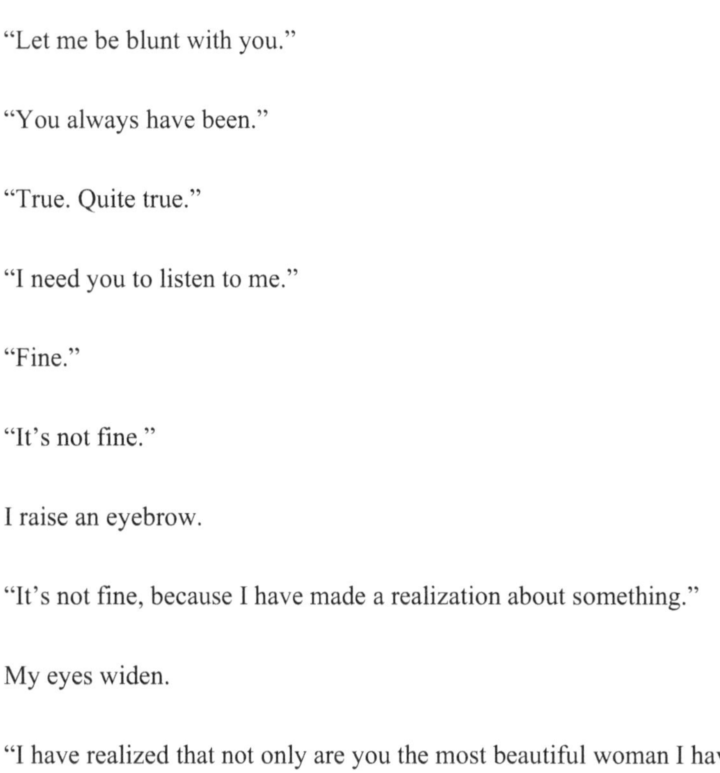

“Let me be blunt with you.”

“You always have been.”

“True. Quite true.”

“I need you to listen to me.”

“Fine.”

“It’s not fine.”

I raise an eyebrow.

“It’s not fine, because I have made a realization about something.”

My eyes widen.

“I have realized that not only are you the most beautiful woman I have ever had the pleasure to lay my eyes on or my body, frankly. But besides that, I have decided that I do not want our agreement to end.”

“You don’t?”

“No. Hear me out. Besides your beauty, which will fade, as we both know, I have found that I take great pleasure in your intelligence and wit and your zest for life. In short, I enjoy your company, Miss Hundine. And…”

He drops to one knee and pulls a black velvet box from his back pocket. He opens it, and there before me is the most beautiful sapphire and diamond ring.

“…because of that, I don’t want to be without you. We share many interests together, and therefore, I have decided that I want to marry you. I am very fond of you, and I feel that I have come so far as to say that I feel love for you. Will you marry me, Miss Hundine?”

My hand flutters to my mouth. My heart thumps a wild beat, and I emit an utterly, unladylike cry. “No.”

His face falls.

“I mean. I can’t believe this. You want to marry me? I thought our agreement was ending. What I mean to say is that, I am fond of you too and I didn’t want our arrangement to end either. I never thought I wanted to be married, but if it means waking up to your considerable assets, I feel that I do want to do this. But are you sure about this?”

“You caused my heart to stop beating for a moment, Miss Hundine. The proper answer to a bloke asking you to marry him, if you love him, would be ‘yes’.”

“You are sure.”

“Absolutely sure Miss Hundine. Never more sure in my life.”

“Well then the matter is settled. I say yes to your proposal, but you are never allowed to tell me what to do, unless it is in the bedroom. And even then, I have a right to change my mind.”

“That sounds just like the Miss Hundine that I have come to know and love.” He smiles, and stands, slips the delicate ring on my finger and grabs my waist, pulling me to him in a passionate embrace. I start laughing.

“I wasn’t expecting this. I thought you were going to end our agreement.”

He chuckles. “I surprised the both of us. I think it just took meeting the right woman. That would be you, Miss Hundine.”

Another couple stroll past, and we break apart.

“I was going to wait until next week, but I couldn’t wait any longer.”

“I see.”

“You say I talk too much. And I do. But I want you to know, that I have begun to change my views of women, especially you.”

I raise my eyebrow.

“I have been hard on women.”

I nod.

“Too hard, perhaps.”

The corner of my mouth raises slightly. He’s serious.

“You have schooled me, Miss Hundine. And for that I am grateful.”

“I’m not a traditional woman, Professor Heimdahl.”

“Call me Henry.”

“As you wish Henry. I have a great desire to learn things that only men have access to.”

“I think I have shown you that I am quite willing to give you access to my manhood.”

I roll my eyes, but I can’t help the smile that follows, meeting his wide grin with my own.

He reaches into his jacket and pulls out some papers. He hands them to me.

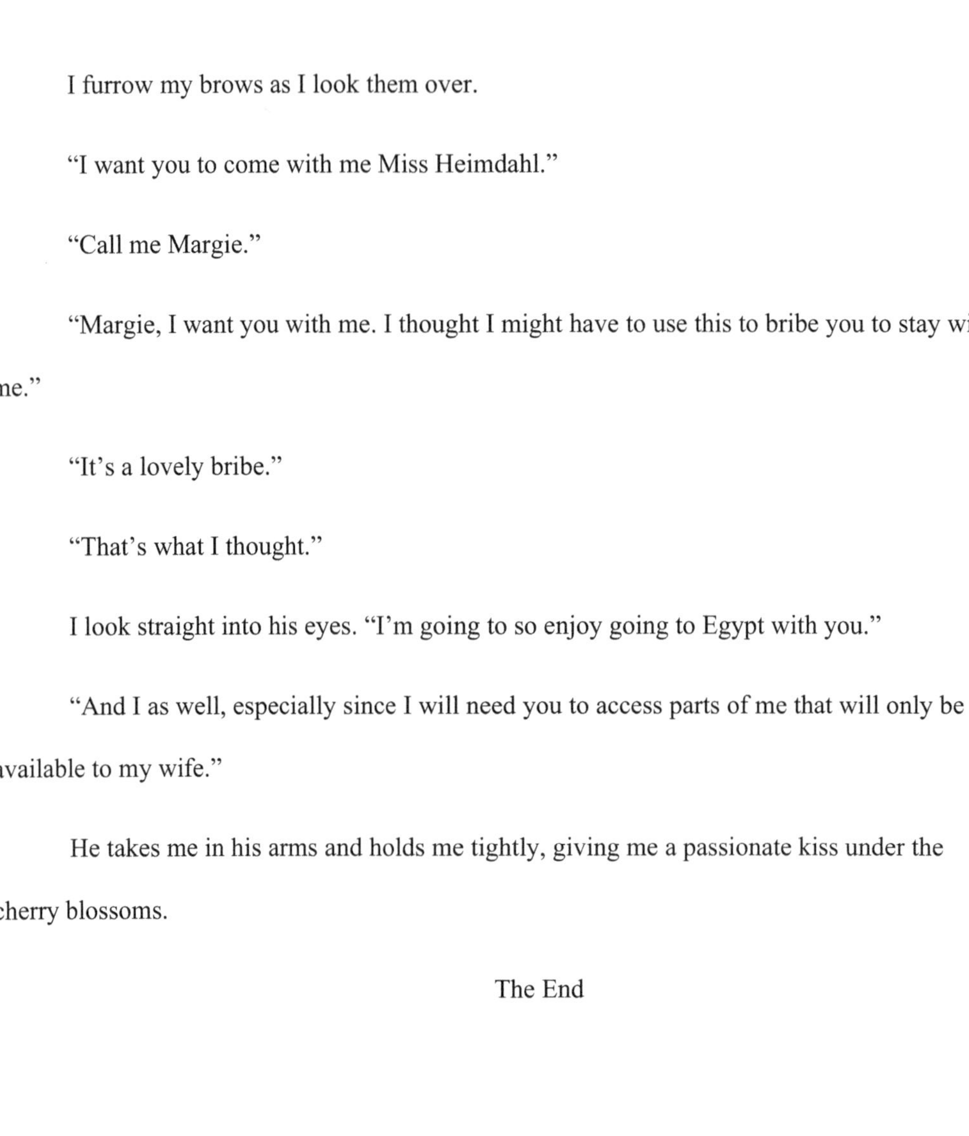

I furrow my brows as I look them over.

"I want you to come with me Miss Heimdahl."

"Call me Margie."

"Margie, I want you with me. I thought I might have to use this to bribe you to stay with me."

"It's a lovely bribe."

"That's what I thought."

I look straight into his eyes. "I'm going to so enjoy going to Egypt with you."

"And I as well, especially since I will need you to access parts of me that will only be available to my wife."

He takes me in his arms and holds me tightly, giving me a passionate kiss under the cherry blossoms.

The End

Want something longer? What follows is an excerpt from BENEATH THE BILLIONAIRE, a full length, steamy, contemporary romance novel.

Beneath The Billionaire

By

Jessie Knight

Text Copyright©2021 by Jessie Knight

No part of this publication may be reproduced, distributed, or transmitted in any form or by any means, electronic or otherwise, without the express written consent of the author, except in the case of brief quotations for the purpose of book reviews.

This book is a work of fiction. All names, character, locations, and incidents are products of the author's imagination. Any semblance to actual persons or situations is entirely coincidental.

Chapter 1

Valentin

So, the day Mother Nature decides to unleash her fury with an early spring blizzard is the day I meet HER. But I'm getting ahead of myself.

It's been a hell of a winter, and I haven't been socializing that much with anyone other than the crew that works for my company and my household manager, Señora Madora.

Señora Madora is a lovely woman, and a self-proclaimed psychic. Think Teresa Caputo with a Spanish accent. And around the same time last year, she predicted that in a year I would meet the love of my life and some other things which are too embarrassingly strange to even think about. Señora Madora was very specific, said the woman I'd meet would be blond, blue eyed, and young. The young part is completely not my type BTW; I've never dated a woman younger than myself, too much drama for my tastes. Part of me knows that Señora Madora told me those things trying to push me to get back on the horse again.

But I find myself standing here, fueling my truck and I get this hair prickling, electric tingling kind of thing go down my spine, and when I look up, I see a real-life Goddess. The first thing I notice is the attitude, second, she's wearing combat boots and with her hair whipping about her face, she looks like a force of nature to be reckoned with.

She's not from around here. That much I can tell by the NC license plate. Doesn't have snow tires on her jeep, and we're about to get a blizzard. What the hell is she doing out here in this weather? She looks completely out of place, and that's an understatement.

Why is this girl not dressed for the weather? No sign of skiis, and all's she's wearing is a hoodie and ripped jeans. Her hair is crazy long and straight and blows all over the fucking place as she steps out of her jeep. She tucks her hoodie to her, and I catch a glimpse of her curves beneath the shapeless fabric. I do love curves on a woman.

My eyes stay on her, as she walks in my direction, silently willing her to look at me. She does, her eyes startling as she catches my eyes on her.

Our eyes lock for a moment and a blush races across her face. She drops eye lock, grabs the fuel nozzle, and jams it into the side of her car. I study her car, reminded of Señora Madora's predictions that the woman would be from the south. My eyes return to her, and I catch her staring at me. She stills for a moment, as my eyes indicate to her that I know she was staring at me, the wind aggressively whips her long hair across her face. It's an expressive face, one with vivid blue angelic eyes, sensuous pouty lips, and flaxen hair.

She wraps one arm about her middle, trying to stem off the cold with her barely there hoodie that keeps falling off one shoulder. I am sorely tempted to offer her my jacket, but I know she wouldn't take it, I can tell by her demeanor.

Her phone jangles again and before I can say a word to her, she takes off at a clip towards the convenience store, a scowl plastered across her expressive face. I don't need to go in, but I'm going to discover her name, and find out about her.

Would I be doing this if Señora Madora had not made any predictions? Yes. Why? Her damned bold attitude. Her aliveness. Maybe even her strangeness. Lucky for me she doesn't know who's coming for her.

Chapter 2

Anna

The air is a frigid 28 degrees Fahrenheit and the wind blustery, as I pull into a gas station in Newport, Vermont, a couple miles south of the Canadian border. I should have gotten my winter jacket out of the back of my jeep before I stepped out, but I left balmy North Carolina at 70 degrees and the brief stops I made along the way didn't require it. If there was any sleepiness in me before, that is completely dissipated by the blast of wind that hits me square in the face.

Technically, we just passed the vernal equinox, but it doesn't look like spring has sprung here, nor does it look imminent. More like, winter has not yet departed. Not that I mind, since I want to try my hand at skiing, for the first time ever. It would have made sense for me to have checked the weather before I left home, but sometimes my impulsive side takes over the decision-making process, and I was in a hurry to get up here.

Pulling my hoodie tighter to me, I walk around my jeep to the fuel pump, catching a glimpse of an extremely tall, broad shouldered man across from me. The wind takes this moment to catch my hair and viciously rend it across my face, as my eyes lock with the dark, bold gaze of the most strikingly handsome man I have ever laid eyes on.

God have mercy on my soul.

I catch my breath and glance down at my borrowed boots, making sure I don't trip over the concrete island between us. *Player or taken*, logic brain informs me.

Logic or not, *he is sinfully fine*, all chiseled cheeks and stubbly jawline, and well dressed for the weather, a sign of intelligence. Drives an expensive truck, that's an indication of someone who works hard. Other hard things come to mind, *playing hard,* there's that.

Nope. Player or taken. Logic brain is frequently a killjoy.

Maybe I was imagining that he was staring at me. Ignoring the phone jangling in my pocket, I reach for the handle of the fuel hose and insert it into my jeep's tank, distractedly not realizing that I should have swiped my card first. Logic is overruled by instinct, and my gaze impulsively flicks to Mr. Handsome, as I wait for the fuel to dispense.

I get a jolt, as I realize he's staring, his dark, shrewd eyes clearly fixed in my direction. Stupidly, my heart does a flip flop, my cheeks reddening under his scrutiny, as the ferocious wind takes my hair and relentlessly whips it across my face. I drop gaze to my oversized, black steel-toes, my heart beginning to hammer in my chest, like a gazelle under the watchful gaze of a ravenous lion.

I want to look at him again, but my phone keeps ringing. For the second time, I hit the side button, and it stops the noise.

I risk another look at him. His attention is on placing the fuel nozzle back in its slot, but it immediately comes back to me, and my heart jumps again. That was deliberate. He wants to catch me looking at him. He stares at me in a more pointed way this time, as if to say, make sure you know that I caught you looking at me.

Time comes to a standstill for a moment as I get sucked into those eyes. Dark demon like eyes that don't miss anything in their environment. There's an essence about him that exudes power and confidence, and potentially perilous aggression, giving me the impression that if there was something before him that he wanted, he would take it.

He doesn't break his gaze with me and neither does he smile flirtatiously or anything, just stares at me with hunger in his eyes. Studies me like a predator would, and that thought, for some reason, sends a curious thrill down my spine.

My phone goes off for the third time, and I realize that the pump is not accepting my credit card for whatever reason. Reluctantly, I break eye lock with the handsome stranger and begin to walk towards the convenience shop, sliding my finger across my phone to accept the incoming call.

"Mom, I told you already. I'll be fine." Do not. I repeat, do not, send someone to check on me." My exasperation rises as my mother's insistent voice broadcasts though my cell phone.

Crossing the service station at a snappy pace, I try to ignore the bitterly cold wind swirling around me. My mother is a perpetual 'fixer' and sensing that I might be in over my head in this northern clime far from home and about to experience my first ever, real life blizzard, she's been calling around the area to see if any of Nana's old friends can offer me assistance.

"Anna, darling, I already asked, the Bennett's will stop by the cabin to check in with you. I don't think Nana's cabin is equipped for a blizzard. You will be out in the middle of nowhere by yourself, what if you lose power? Nana didn't have a generator as far as I'm aware."

"Mom! There's a fireplace. Now, stop worrying, I can handle it all myself. I have to go." It was a 16-hour drive from North Carolina to Vermont, and I'm counting down the stops before I can reach my newly inherited log cabin. Beat and annoyed, I head inside to pay, hoping that my credit card doesn't give me any more trouble.

It is.

"I'm sorry, you're going to have to pay in cash." The service attendant, sporting pink frosted hair tips, a lip piercing and cracking a large wad of gum looks at me expectantly. She doesn't look a bit sorry for this at all.

I quickly begin to rummage through my purse. "I don't understand why my card won't work here."

The attendant shrugs her shoulders.

My face heats, as a giant line begins to form behind me. I suppose everyone wants a fill up before the blizzard hits full force. I really should have gotten more cash out of the bank before I drove up here. "All I have is a five." It's not going to get me up and down the mountain. "Is there an ATM around here?"

She cracks her gum and looks at my five. "The nearest ATM is that way about 5 blocks. I'm not sure if the ATM is working right now. Do you want five dollars in gas?"

I sigh and brush my hair off my face. "Yes. Sure."

"Here." The handsome dude, that I was eyeing moments ago at the pump, steps forward and lays a fifty-dollar bill on the counter.

Blood rushes to my face. My eyes search upwards towards the face of a-god-come-to-earth, who has just offered to help me out. Oh. Wow. He does smile. His laugh lined eyes search mine with such kindness, that momentarily I'm speechless, my irritation dropping away like mist parting before the morning sun.

"Long way from home?" He smiles at me, and my heart skips a beat. Obviously, he's been listening in on the conversation and my southern drawl.

My pulse ramps, and my face continues to heat against my will. "I am, but you don't have to do this. I'm sure there's an ATM around here somewhere."

"Don't worry about it, I insist." His deep voice emanates a rugged sexiness and has the trace of what sounds like a Russian accent.

I hesitate. People continue to stare, and my cheeks indicate that an inferno has been ignited at the surface of my skin. I hate it when I blush like this in front of a bunch of people. "Thank you so much." My voice sounds higher than normal, as I thank him.

"My pleasure."

A wave of lightheadedness passes over me at the masculine rumble of his voice. The blush stays with me until I get back into my jeep. It isn't till I get there, that I realize I have completely lost my manners. I should have asked him his name and offered to pay him back, but I'd been too flustered to even think of it. Hands shaking slightly, I insert the key in the ignition, sit back and exhale.

The mystery man leaves the store, holding the door open for an attractive woman in a designer coat and boots. Self-consciously, I run a hand though my hair and look down at my paint splattered skinny jeans, wool socks, and engineer treads that I borrowed from my friend's brother that are about 3 sizes too big. No wonder that man took pity on me, I look like hell. I guess that was why he was staring at me.

I've only slept for about a half an hour in the last 18 hours. Not that it matters anyway, I didn't ask him his name, and by the looks of it, he probably has a wife or a girlfriend. My gaze stays on him and the pretty lady. The pair are in deep conversation, and then the woman touches the sleeve of his coat in an affectionate gesture.

I look away, not wanting to be caught staring at them. What am I thinking anyway? I'm here for a vacation. There isn't time to begin a relationship. But something stirs inside me, something I haven't felt in a long time.

Pushing aside thoughts of the generous mystery man, I grudgingly turn back to business at hand. I need to call the credit card company and find a bank, in addition to all the other things I need to get before I head up to Nana's cabin. Shifting my car into gear, I pull out of the gas station and onto the main road, watching the mystery man and lady in my rearview mirror.

The snow, which had merely been flurries at the station is beginning to fall harder, and I turn on my wipers so I can see. It starts to lay on the road, as I meander around the city of Newport, looking for the closest bank with an ATM. An hour later, I finish with banking and shopping for supplies. A forty-five-minute drive to my cabin lies ahead, and I turn the dial on the radio searching for an update on the weather.

I find one. *"Looks like we're gonna get a big one folks. The National Weather Service is calling for record snowfalls, as much as 48 inches. Don't go out if you don't have to and keep warm. Stay with us for updates."*

My phone buzzes. I'm expecting it to be my Mom, and I answer without looking at the incoming number, so that I can keep my eyes on the road.

"Mom." My tone is sharp. She needs to relax and stop bugging me.

A sweet-sounding voice is on the other end of the line. "No, I'm afraid not dear. This is Emma Bennett. Is this Anna Anderson?"

"Yes, this is Anna."

"Anna, I'm an old friend of your Grandmother's. Your mother just called me to say that you will be in the area for a while, and my husband Harold and I were wondering if you would like to stay with us for a few days until the snow is cleared out. Your Grandmother's cabin is quite a way out from town, and they don't always plow the roads up there on the mountain. I know your mother is very worried about you, she said you have never been up north during the winter season. She rambles on, seeming to anticipate my thoughts. "And I know it's officially spring, but up here, it can act like winter until May."

I know she means well, but my irritation rises at the mention of my meddling mother.

"I appreciate your invite Mrs. Bennett, but I'll be fine. I have the fireplace if the power goes out."

"I thought as much. I can see that you take after your Grandmother. She was very independent too. I just want to warn you that if we get the 4 feet of snow that the weatherman is predicting that you may be stuck on the side of that mountain for days my dear."

"Please don't worry about me. I have everything I need, and I'm alright with being alone. This is a vacation for me."

Emma pauses. "Okay dear. But just to humor an old lady, would it be alright if we sent a friend of the family by to check on you this afternoon?" It's more of a statement than a question, I realize as Emma continues. "His name is Valentin Tsarev. We call him 'the Tsar.' It's our nickname for him." Mrs. Bennett chuckles, and I silently raise my eyebrows at the nickname. "It would make us feel so much better, if we knew you were safe during the storm."

"I don't want to make anyone go out of their way for me Mrs. Bennett. I can assure you, I'll be fine, really."

"Oh, it's not out of his way at all, dear. He lives right up the road from you. He has a logging business on the mountain. You see? It's no trouble at all," she says cheerfully. "We already talked to him about you."

I try to leave the rising annoyance out of my voice. After all, Mrs. Bennett is simply being neighborly. But all I want right now is a hot shower and a nap. "I see. It's not necessary, but if you insist. What time will he be stopping by?"

"Later this afternoon dear."

"Thank you for calling Mrs. Bennett."

"You're quite welcome. Please come and visit us after the storm has passed, we'd love to meet you."

"Of course, I look forward to meeting you." I hang up and consider calling my mother to tell her to stop interfering, but instead, I allow my attention to drift to the sight of the thick, gently falling snowflakes and the beauty of the snow-covered Green Mountains in the distance.

When at last my jeep begins its long trek up the road that leads to Nana's cabin, I inhale. The view is breathtaking. Enormous snow-covered pines line the path, and as I rumble down the road, a pond comes into view. I pull into the driveway of a cozy looking log cabin, cut the engine, and open my door to a big gust of wind. Tramping through the snow, I head for the cabin.

My heart jumps in anticipation, I place the key in the lock and open the solid wooden door. A rustic wooden table with two chairs sits in the middle of a tidy little kitchen, and a few copper pots hang from the ceiling. There's a cast iron griddle on the stove, and the sink is old fashioned, but I note with relief that is has a faucet with running water. There's a small fridge and some dusty blue Wedgewood teacups on the corner shelf nearby.

Anxious to see the rest of the house, I carry my large duffel bag into the tiny bedroom off the kitchen. The bedroom consists of a double bed, an antique trunk at the foot of the bed, a hand painted dresser in red, and a small army green nightstand on which stands a single dried rose in a crystal bud vase. I throw my duffel on the bed and place a large stack of reading material on top of the dusty nightstand. From the look of things, I'm going to have to give this place a solid cleaning before I settle in.

The bathroom has an old-fashioned toilet, a claw footed tub, over which is a sky light, and a white porcelain sink with an oval mirror. The nicest room is the moderate sized living room with a large stone fireplace and hearth. A gigantic picture window allows me to take in the spectacular view of the mountains in the distance and the pond and snow-covered trees that sit below the level of the cabin. The walls are a warm cedar and contrast to the grey skies and snow, which continues to fall.

I hug myself and feel a twinge of excitement shoot through me despite the long journey to get here. It's perfect. No Wi-Fi, no cell service. Peace.

I tie my unruly hair into a ponytail, crank the heat to warm the cabin, turn on my portable radio and set to work. First on the agenda is the bathroom, which I speedily scour while fantasizing about the long hot soak I'm taking after I finish with the rest of the house. Moving onto the living room, I peel the sheets off the furniture, revealing a worn leather sofa and 2 tufted leather club chairs. The coffee table is made of natural polished wood on which sits some old National Geographic magazines and a faded ivory candle on a wooden plank.

I pause at the fireplace mantel, looking at the cluster of family pictures. I smile as I look at the picture of Nana and Pop on their wedding day, an awful one of myself in second grade, sporting a toothless, crooked smile, my Mom and Stepdad on a cruise, and Uncle Jack in his Navy uniform.

I reach for a picture of Nana in Peru. She lost Pop when she was 40, and after that she traveled a lot. I always admired her for being an adventurer. I hold her picture to my heart. "I miss you Nana." As I speak, a shaft of sunlight breaks through the storm clouds and hits me in the face. I hold the picture and look at her face again, memories streaming in with the sun.

"Live life on your own terms Anna." Nana's words come back to me.

"I am Nana. At least. I'm trying too."

The sun disappears and the room darkens with the storm. I turn up the volume on the radio. Singing along to the music helps me work a little faster, and after I mop the wide planked wood flooring, I do a little dance in front of the picture window.

"You never close your eyes anymore, when you kiss my lips." My can of dusting polish becomes my microphone. Because, who cares? No one is here to see me look like a fool. A surge of happiness shoots through me. The place is starting to look spotless, and it's so cozy. I love it! Tonight, I'm doing nothing but sitting by the fire and reading and relaxing. That's my plan anyway.

Chapter 3

Anna

While waiting for the tub to fill, I strip off my ratty jeans and t-shirt and throw a handful of salt crystals into the tub. A cloud of steam arises from the bath, and I sink gratefully into the tub, enjoying the steamy heat against my skin. My muscles start to unknot themselves, and I lie back and close my eyes, daydreaming. At last. It's so peaceful here. Not a sound, except for the swish of the wind blowing through the pines outside the log walls, and the indiscernible sound of snow gently falling on the tin roof.

Lifting my feet to the edge of the tub, I scoot my body forward, and allow the hot water to soak into my scalp. Snowflakes drift over the skylight and I get lost in a stare, mesmerized by the beauty. Thoughts idling, I wonder how my business partner is making out. I trust Tim, he's a capable person, and lucky. Tim and his wife have the perfect little family, in love with each other and their new baby.

Not to be left out of the thought parade, my inner cynic injects her own thought. *Dream on Anna.* What Tim and Mia have belongs in a fairy tale. After my last breakup, well, so much for fairy tales. Amid my reverie, I'm lifted from delicious solitude by a loud knock at the kitchen door.

OMG. I forgot that Mrs. Bennett's friend was going to stop by. *Crap.*

It's gotta be '*the Tsar.*' I'd love to disregard it, as the timing can't be more inconvenient. But if I ignore it, he'll probably speak with the Bennett's, who'll speak with my mother and then who knows what will happen? Knowing my mother, she'll call the police. Not to mention, it's obvious I'm here because my jeep is parked outside, and since I already told Mrs. Bennett that it's okay for the man to stop by, I better get up. Otherwise, I risk being rude to my new neighbors.

"Awesome timing." I mutter. The knocking becomes a pounding.

"I'm coming." I yell, wondering if the man can even hear me through the thick walls. The last thing I want to do is get out of this steamy bath. My dirty clothes lie mangled on the floor, and I make the hasty decision against throwing them back on, maybe it will give him a strong hint that I'm otherwise occupied.

My mother's voice resounds in my head, "Now Anna, remember, good southern girls always dress for company, no matter who it is." Screw that. I'm on vacation. And I'm lacking sleep, and clearly, manners.

I hastily throw my bath towel around me, stride to the door, and fling it open, expecting a much older man than the one that stands before me wielding an enormous bouquet of flowers and eyeing me with a bemused expression.

My heart literally skips a beat. I grip the door handle for assistance, feeling like the impulsive idiot that I sometimes am. Here before me is the ruggedly handsome dude from the gas station who I had some serious eye lock with and who generously paid for my fuel. Momentarily confused, I clutch my towel for support, as my body, traitor that it is, sends a blush traveling over every inch of my skin.

The name Emma Bennett gave me had sounded Russian, and this man has a Russian accent. Therefore, it is highly likely that 'the Tsar' is standing before me.

Without thinking, I cheekily cock an eyebrow at him and blurt out, "You're the Bennett's friend, 'the Tsar' I presume?"

He gives me a sexy smile, "Obviously, you've spoken with Emma."

"She warned me," I smile, oblivious to the cold and feeling like my annoyance has dissipated at the sound of his deep, accented voice.

"And you're my new neighbor, Ms. Anna Andersen. I did not realize this earlier, or I would have introduced myself at the gas station."

"Yes. Please call me Anna. Thank you again. That was exceedingly kind of you. I'll pay you back."

He glances at my towel, an apologetic expression on his face. "Not necessary. But I've come at an inconvenient time. I would have called, but Emma said you don't have a phone installed. I'll stop by later."

Whoa. He's assertive. He isn't asking. The memory of the eye lock experience at the gas station returns, he struck me as a man not afraid to go after what he wants. But now he's all charming and such. Hmmm.

"It's not necessary, really. I'm fine. I'm sorry to have wasted your time. The Bennett's are worried for nothing."

His dark eyes assess me with a frankness that makes me feel naked. He's looking at me like I'm an unnatural specimen that doesn't belong out here in this seeming wilderness, as though I need protection from myself.

"I'll stop by later Anna." The low rumble of his masculine voice and the forcefulness of his demeanor sends a tingling sensation straight to my belly. "These are for you. Welcome to the neighborhood." He hands me an exotic bouquet of multicolored blooms.

I reach for the bouquet, making a grab for my towel, as it slides dangerously towards my backside. Another blush rushes across my cheeks as our fingers graze each other. "Thank you, these are beautiful, but I don't know if I'll be here later."

"You're welcome. I'll see you around 4 Anna. If you're still here that is. I have a proposal for you." He calls over his shoulder to me as he heads for his truck.

I shut the door against the swirling snow, plop the flowers onto the kitchen table and watch his truck drive down the road. A strange mixture of feelings swirl through my body. Who is this man? Insistent, forceful. Handsome as hell. Not like anyone I've ever met in the south. Probably married, engaged or with someone. The woman dressed to the nines at the gas station seemed friendly with him.

I assure myself that the only reason he's returning is to satisfy the Bennett's that I'm okay. The proposal means he is probably going to try and convince me to stay with the Bennett's during the storm. But that's my luck. My friend Rachel claims it's because I have a tainted view of men. Of course, we did do some intense staring at the gas station, but…

Scenes from what seem like a lifetime ago flash before my gaze. Jason, my former boyfriend, turning in shock as I enter his apartment. Him naked, mounting a girl from behind on the sofa near the door. The sofa we'd made out on. The shock wave that came over me with the realization that he was fucking someone else on the day that I was ready to have sex with him for the first time.

Wearing nothing but the sexiest set of black lingerie under my trench coat and a pair of stilettos, I ran out of the apartment, hearing Jason's rueful voice calling my name. All the planning to make it the *best ever*. I'd wanted everything to be perfect for our first time. I wanted to surprise him. Well, it sure as hell did. It was humiliating.

From that point on, I'd barely looked at guys, but it made me driven enough to start my own business with one of my best friends and depressed enough to lose the extra forty pounds I'd been carrying around since my parent's divorce.

Returning to the present, I stare at the flowers. They're gorgeous. When is the last time I received flowers like this from a man? Never, honestly. Not like this. They're so artfully arranged, I'm sure they come from a flower shop. Leaning over the arrangement, I pluck out the attached note.

Dear Anna,

Please accept this welcome to Vermont. Your Grandmother was a wonderful neighbor, and she is missed by all in these parts. Do not hesitate to ask if there is any assistance you might need.

Best Regards,

Valentin Tsarev

I gape at the note, wondering about the man I've just met. He is a gentleman. Older than me, the laugh lines around his eyes betray that fact. But, for an older man, he is quite nice to behold. I remind myself that a man like this is most likely not single. Not that I care. I've sworn off the male gender. For my own good, of course. The staring incident? Maybe he thought I looked like hell because, I did. Who doesn't after being cooped up in a car for 16 hours?

I return to the tub. The water is still hot, but I top it off with more until all I can see is a haze of steam. Closing my eyes, I review the shock I felt when I opened the door. I'd been expecting a rough old, grizzled mountain man, not the bold figure that stood before me with the piercing eyes and commanding features. He is amazing to behold, more so because he seems like a genuinely kind person. I remind myself that I saw him talking with a beautiful woman. Not only that, his reason for returning is benign, likely due to the Bennett's via my mother's request.

My logical self tells me to stop fantasizing and that the best course of action is to make sure that I'm not here when he returns. There isn't going to be anymore pestering about me being able to stay in this lovely little cabin while the storm rides itself out. End of story. And I'm not going to allow myself to feel a crazed attraction for him, despite the staring between us. He's overtly bold and pushy. And kind, my better side speaks up, and then the devil side wins out. *Forget it*, it whispers.

I lather myself up, wash my hair, and shave off the stubble. Stepping out, I leave a trail of water droplets across the floor and towel off in front of the fire. It's so refreshing to be clean. I sit naked on the fur rug and enjoy the warmth of the fire on my bare back. The snow falls thickly out of a slate gray sky, intensely beautiful. Once I'm warm and dry, I cream my legs and slip into my favorite old jeans, a black T shirt, hoodie, and a pair of fuzzy socks.

Glad for the engineer boots I borrowed, I throw on my jacket and head to the shed for more wood. It takes me about an hour to stack enough wood next to the fireplace to feel satisfied that I won't be needing anymore for several days. Then, I bring the shovel into the kitchen, thinking it might be handy if the snow piles up near the door.

My tasks finished, I check my cell for the time, noting the no service icon. 3:33 PM. Time to head out before the Tsar gets back. Rummaging around, I find tape and an envelope, and set about writing a thank you note to the Tsar with $50 included. I tape it to the inside door of the kitchen, grab my jacket and winter things, and head for my Jeep. I'll take a drive, find a place to pull over, and hike. Oddly enough, I can hear my friend Rachel's voice making a clucking sound in my head. Rachel would not approve, she'd bug me to take a chance, but I'm not taking a chance on someone that most certainly has a special someone, especially when I'm only here for a few weeks.

It's extraordinarily gorgeous, the thickly frosted pines and deeply drifted snow make it look like an enchanted forest. Quite a change from the southern climate I'm used to in North Carolina. We rarely get snow that far south. This is something I always wanted to see when I was a kid.

I direct my Jeep down the snow-covered dirt road that runs past the cabin. After a short drive, I find an overlook, pull off the road and park my Jeep. The wind is picking up, and it bites at my cheeks, as I get out of the shelter of my vehicle and head down the road. Snow lies thickly on the road surface, only visible in a few bare patches where the wind has sliced it away.

Determinedly, I trudge along, pausing to take pictures of the winter wonderland before me. A logging truck rumbles past, and the driver waves and nods at me like he knows me. After 30 minutes of walking, a sign looms ahead of me. Tsarev Logging Company, Inc.

Surprised, I make a hasty U turn towards my Jeep. I've been trying to avoid the man, not run into him! As I turn, the wind catches at my face, taking my breath away. Somehow, the walk back towards my Jeep feels much colder than the walk away from it. A red Chevy pickup passes me, followed by two cars. Probably workers, I think, maybe leaving early because of the storm.

Five minutes later, a black F-450 pulls alongside. My pulse begins to race, I recognize the truck. The window lowers, and the Tsar's handsome face appears, looking amused. Does he think I'm here to check him out?

"Enjoying the weather Anna?" Brows lift, dark eyes absorb me, head to foot.

For some stupid reason, the second I look at him, I trip on a chunk of ice, twisting my ankle in the process, and fall headlong into the road. Pain flashes through my ankle, as I lie sprawled out like a roadkill.

Are you kidding me right now? Why in God's name did I have to fall in front of a man that looks at me like that?

The Tsar stops his truck, jumps out and swiftly moves to my side. I pull myself to a sitting position, feeling incredibly awkward and stupid. It's these damned oversized boots. That and the feeling that I'm going to faint every time I have an encounter with this man.

"Anna, are you alright?" He touches my arm gently.

My face flushes crimson, and it isn't the cold. "I'm OK, I just twisted my ankle."

"I'm going to lift you up. Put your arm around my neck."

I follow his instructions, expecting him to lift me to my feet, but he doesn't bother with that option. His steely arms lift me and carry me to his truck.

Not that I'm a stick by any stretch of the imagination, but he moves with me as though I weigh next to nothing. Heart rate accelerating, I catch the heady, masculine scent of his cologne. Somehow, I've died and gone to heaven. He's all man, from the hard sinews of his arms to the muscular frame of his body, that I can't help but feel, despite the winter coats between us.

He places me on the seat. "I'm going to drive you home and look at it."

"If you could please just drop me off at my Jeep, it's down the road from here."

"I'll have one of my men drive it home for you. I'll call now. Here give me your keys."

"I can drive myself. It's not far."

"No worries. We're your neighbors, let us give you a hand."

I hand my keys to him, wondering if he is going to insist that I stay with the Bennett's. Of course, he is. In the past four hours, he has been there to give me money, a neighborly greeting, and a lift in his truck. I look out of my element here, and I know it.

I spend most of the ride back to the cabin wondering if the Tsar thinks I'm a complete idiot. The very thing I tried to avoid has happened. He pulls into the driveway. My Jeep follows, driven by one of his men, and another follows in a pickup. This is unbelievably embarrassing.

Expecting to hobble into the house on my own, I get ready to slide out of the truck, my cheeks flaming scarlet from all the attention. The Tsar is quicker, and he scoops me off the seat into his arms, and heads for the kitchen door. I thank the men that have returned my Jeep, feeling my face heat into what I am sure looks a four-alarm inferno, when the Tsar refuses to put me down. He insists on carrying me inside and gives me a surprised look when I tell him that door is unlocked.

"You shouldn't leave your house unlocked." He chastises me, as he sets me on the kitchen chair, pulling the other one under my bad ankle. "Even though it is rather desolate around here, there have still been the occasional break-ins. It's not safe for a woman alone." He looks into my eyes, searching to see if I am taking him seriously.

"I really do know how to take care of myself, Valentin." I give him an exasperated sigh, preparing for him to suggest that I stay elsewhere during the storm.

He laughs, and then says with a twinkle in his eye, "Is that why you fell in front of my truck, because you were taking care of yourself?"

"Thanks for that. I was having a clumsy moment. Alright, laugh. Yes, it was funny."

"I'm teasing you." He pulls up a chair and gently takes my foot in his strong, capable looking hands. "I think we should take a look at your ankle." He pulls off my boot and sock and looks from my boot to my foot, giving me a knowing smile. "Your boyfriend's?"

My cheeks flush at the question. "No. I borrowed them from my friend's brother. He has big feet."

"Compared to yours, yes. Good God woman. No wonder you tripped." He chuckles as he probes my ankle gently with his fingers.

I can't help but notice how large his hands are. "Ow! That's the spot."

"You're lucky, I think it is not sprained, just badly bruised. Do you have ice or frozen peas?"

"No." I look at him ruefully. "I wasn't expecting to need it."

"Ziploc bags?"

"Yeah." I point to the cupboard.

The Tsar grabs one, heads outside and fills it with snow and places the snow filled baggie on my ankle. "That should help with the swelling."

"Thank you, neighbor," I give him a cautious smile, amazed at how kind he is, but waiting for his 'proposal'. It's coming, I know it is. He's a considerate man, he'd probably offer to drive me to the Bennett's and pick me up if I asked.

"My pleasure." He gives me a warm look that sends tingles up my spine.

"And you wanted to ask me something?"

He gives me an apologetic look. "Anna, I think you should stay with the Bennett's until the storm is over. That way I will know you are safe." There it is. I pegged it.

"Absolutely not, I am perfectly fine here on my own."

"It's not uncommon for the power to go out on this mountain during snowstorms, and you'll be left without heat. "

"I thought of that. But I brought enough wood in for the fireplace to last at least two days."

"Anna, the power could be out for a week. And you will not be able to bathe either." The corners of his eyes crinkle with his smile, and I feel sure he is remembering me standing at the door in a towel.

"Valentin, I appreciate your concern, but I am fine here by myself. Seriously."

"If I can't convince you to stay with the Bennett's would you at least agree to coming with me to dine at my home tonight?"

My heart feels like it's going to leap out of my chest.

"You can meet Señora Madora and have one good meal before you are forced to cook over your fireplace for a week. She is the best cook on this side of the mountain." My heart does a dive at the mention of Señora, but judging by the look on his face, he isn't going to take 'no' for an answer.

"What time?"

"I'll bring you there now. It will save you straining your ankle further."

I'm amazed, I've never met such a determined man. He's obviously used to getting his way. "You like to get your way, don't you?"

"I do. I am known as 'the Tsar' by my friends for a reason."

I see the gleam in his eye when he says this, and I laugh despite myself. "Mrs. Bennett mentioned that. You are a wicked Tsar?" I cock an eyebrow at him.

"Sometimes, but only when necessary." His dark eyes, momentarily serious, examine my lighter ones, sending an electric jolt down my spine. It reminds me of the predatory look he gave me at the gas station.

He turns away, his attention focused out the window. "We should go, it's starting to get dark, and I told Señora Madora we would be back for dinner."

"You told her I was coming?"

"I felt confident that I could persuade you, and I was reasonably sure that you would not agree to stay at the Bennett's. Emma told me that you are very much like your grandmother, an independent woman."

My mouth drops open. Firstly, I thought him arrogant, but he sounded complimentary of my Nana, and that gives me a warm, liquid feeling inside my heart. He is full of surprises.

"I'm going to carry you to my truck. Don't try to fight me." He gives me a wary look that contains a little smile.

A little fluttering sensation kicks around in my belly. He is entirely charming and forceful, and he knows it.

"Put your arm around my shoulders," he commands.

My heart rate accelerates, as I place my arm around his neck and his arms encircle me. His scent and the strength of his body are intoxicating to my senses. The temptation to run my fingers over the dark stubble of his jawline hits me full force, commanding other parts of my body to respond at the pleasurable images that are running through my brain.

With a sigh, I give myself into his steely hold and allow myself to be carried to his truck. He places me on the seat, and I discreetly watch him as he walks around and slides into the driver seat.

"Thank you for everything Valentin."

"You're welcome Anna." A thrill runs through my entire body as he looks into my eyes. The truck rumbles to life under his touch, and we head up the hill to his home. The snow swirls around the truck, enclosing us into what feels like a cave inside the cab.

On the drive to his home, I finally gather enough courage to ask, "Is Señora Madora your wife?"

"Heavens no!" That brings a laugh from him, though I notice that for a split second, pain seems to register on his face at the word 'wife'. "Señora Madora runs the household. You'll like her Anna, she's got a heart of gold, and she knows how to cook."

"She's your maid?"

"I don't think of her that way. She is like family, like a mother figure to me and my men. It works out well."

A barely discernible *Tsarev Logging* sign appears out of nowhere on the left. It's getting hard to see anything at a distance. A road turns off to the left just past the sign. We continue our ascent. Ten minutes later, he turns the wheel to the left and follows a long road to his house. How he's able to see anything, I'm unsure. To my eyes, the road and the landscape are one continuous blur of white.

The mansion is a massive log and stone, three story structure. Double doors stand at the entrance, and wide paned glass windows cover the house. Cypress trees in iron planters stand on either side of the doorway. A smaller but elegant house stands off to the left. Immense maples and pine trees ring the properties. The front door opens, and I see an older, beautiful, dark skinned woman standing there, beaming, and waving. Señora Madora.

Valentin opens the passenger door and scoops me up into his arms before I can protest. The feel of his warm strong arms, his hard body pressed into mine, and the scent of him inebriate my senses. I warn myself to stop, there is not going to be anything between us, there can't be for many reasons. But my body has a will of its own, my pulse races and the light headedness returns.

The snow swirls around us as we make our way to the house, Valentin shouting to the Señora for an ice pack. She disappears into the house, leaving the door wide open for us to enter.

As he crosses the threshold with me, his eyes meet mine and with a devilish smirk, he says the exact thing that has just crossed my mind, "This is like a man with his bride, eh?"

I allow my eyes to connect with his momentarily, and then I drop them, feeling the heat of an entire body blush wash over me, as tingles of electric energy spark from my navel to my thighs. He must know the effect he has on me; my heart is thumping like it's going to burst out of my chest. Fortunately, I am rescued by Señora, who bustles into the Hall with a concerned look on her face. "Everything is ok?" She asks with a heavy Spanish accent.

I open my mouth to respond, but the Tsar is quicker. "She hurt her ankle, I'm going to give her a chair in the sitting room until dinner is ready." He talks, as he strides into the sitting room, and deposits me on the leather sofa that sits opposite of a stone fireplace. He gently lifts my sore ankle onto the leather Ottoman and takes the ice pack from Señora. Placing it on my ankle, he introduces me to the woman. "Anna, this is Señora Madora. Señora Madora, this is Anna."

A look passes between them that I cannot read, and then Señora bends down to shake my hand, looking incredibly pleased. "My Tsar has brought home an Angel."

He replies to Señora Madora, though, his dark eyes burn into mine, "This one's a fallen Angel, Señora Madora, she fell right in front of my truck."

Another body blush comes over me, and I force myself to break my eye lock with Valentin to look at Señora Madora, "That's kind of you to say. Thank you for having me. I'm sorry to trouble you."

"It is no problem." Señora waves her hands. "He never brings home a woman. I always tell him, 'I love to cook. Bring someone home'. But he never does." She rolls her eyes and looks upwards. "Thank God, finally, my prayers have been answered."

"Señora, when will dinner be ready?" Valentin interrupts her rant. It makes me wonder if he is slightly embarrassed, though he shows no signs of flushing.

"A half an hour or so. Do you like salmon?" She asks me.

"I love anything that I don't have to cook myself."

Señora looks from me to the Tsar, "I like her."

I smile and Señora swishes out of the room, singing a little Spanish song to herself.

"Would you like a drink before dinner?" Valentin offers. "I have a very good pinot grigio."

"That sounds good. Yes, I'd love one."

Valentin leaves, and I scan the richly furnished room. An oil painting of a sailing ship in a stormy sea hangs over the fireplace. Two model ships stand on either side of the mantle, as well as a large piece of coral and some giant seashells. Leather club chairs flank the fireplace, and a rug made of what could be alpaca fur gives a warm field to the sitting area. The walls are a rich red color, and the stone of the fireplace spans the entire wall. A fire burns cheerfully in the grate.

My brain takes in the luxurious surroundings and the man responsible for them. I admit to myself that I am surprised by the intensity of my attraction to this man, especially because I have had a cynical streak about most men since my last breakup. Thoughts war inside me. What if Valentin has ulterior motives? Of course, he does. He was flirting with me. If he weren't attracted to me, he wouldn't have made the comment he did when he carried me over the threshold. I must be careful. He's a man used to getting what he wants. I get that vibe from him.

Some sass part of my brain chirps in with, *and what do you want Anna? Good question.*

Chapter 4

Valentin

Fragrant smells emanate from the kitchen. I reach for the bottle of wine on the granite countertop and a couple of glasses. Señora Madora is prepping the salads, but looks over at me, and gives me a smile that speaks volumes.

"I know you want to say something Señora Madora."

"She's here. And she's beautiful just like I told you she'd be. But the outside is the facade. It's the inside, the fire in her, that you will fall for."

I shake my head and give her a half smile. I'm not about to tell her that I feel the heat of attraction with Anna, but I know she knows.

"You don't believe me, but you will. She gives you a baby." There's a stubborn look on her face. I know she wants to believe that for me because she loves me.

"You're too much Señora Madora. You know that's impossible for me." A stabbing pain grips my heart from the mere thought, but I push it away. Facts are facts.

"Things are not impossible in the Spirit world, Valentin. Trust me, I know these things." She turns her back to me and begins singing a song in Spanish. Thankfully, my guest is too far away to hear this snippet of conversation I've just had with Señora Madora. I love my caretaker, but she's a handful and then some. She's either half-cracked or she does have a relationship with the Spirit world. I suspect it may be a little of both.

"Señora."

She turns, dark eyes twinkling. "Yes, Valentin?"

"God help you and your spirit friends should you decide to tell Ms. Andersen anything that you've said to me."

"Don't worry Valentin. There is no need to say anything to Anna. The person that needed to hear it, is you. Because you are a blockheaded man, too caught up in your own head and not willing to trust again. That is why I had to give you the messages from Spirit. It is because you are stubborn. And you needed hope. I know of the pain you hide."

Shaking my head at her, I place the wine and glasses with some cocktail napkins on a tray. She may have a point, I've been told by family members that I'm stubborn, but the finest medical doctors in the country told me I will never be a father, and that is that. The description and timing of Anna is right on, though, it could have been a lucky guess. I'm not privy to the inner workings of Señora's mind.

"It wasn't a lucky guess, Valentin."

"Stop reading my mind Señora."

She laughs when I narrow my eyebrows at her.

"Promise you won't say anything to her."

"I promise nothing. I have my own free will. But there's nothing I could do to change the future. It is fated for you both in this regard."

"We make our own fate Señora Madora."

"Choose to believe what you will." Her lips curve into a little smile, as she continues to prepare our meal.

I walk the hallway towards the sitting room, aware that the storm winds are intensifying. How is it that Señora Madora was right about a woman from 'way down south' as she had told me a year ago? Said she'd soon come into my life during a snowstorm and basically upend it. Said this woman would be my new neighbor, a beautiful blond, blue eyed young woman.

If I'm honest with myself, I must admit it's weird that she got some things right. But Anna has yet to upend my life, and I'm just doing an old friend a favor. At least that's what I've been telling myself.

Emma Bennett called me and told me that Anna's mother was very worried. Said she needed me to help her, and I intend to honor my friend's wishes. I'll make sure Anna is protected from the storm. Our dinner needs to last long enough for her to realize that she's snowed in and must ride out the storm at my mansion. A harmless thing to do to keep her safe. Unfortunately for Anna, she may have just walked into the wolf's lair.

Anna is studying the oil painting above the mantel when I return. Despite the fact, that she's attracted to me, she seems guarded. Perhaps she's in a relationship. I hand her a glass of wine and take a seat in one of the club chairs nearby.

"Thanks." Anna sips at the wine. "This is delicious."

"I'm glad you like it, it's one of my favorites."

"Is it Italian?"

"Yes. It's from a vineyard of one of my friends."

"Nice. You have an international flair? Your name is Russian, your cook is Spanish, and your wine Italian."

"I like domestic products as well, Anna." I wait to see her reaction. She seems nervous and cautious but doesn't miss my innuendo. Anna blushes, her gaze moving to her wine glass and then back to my lips before returning to fix boldly onto mine. I allow my gaze to drift across her sensuous, soft, plump lips, red as her fiery cheeks, before I return to her luminous eyes, framed with black lashes. My cock twitches. What a combination, blushing and bold at the same time.

I like what I see. There's a defiance in her eyes, a liveliness. I rest my jaw on the edge of my fingertips and continue to study her. She unzips her hoodie, allowing me to see what I already know, that she's flushed everywhere.

"I like your oil painting."

"Thank you. That's my father's ship. He was a sea captain."

"Really? That's interesting. Who is the artist?"

"My mother."

"Wow. She's amazing."

"She was."

At that moment, Señora Madora appears and announces that dinner is ready. “I thought you might want to eat in here by the fireplace, so I have prepared your food on two trays. Would that be acceptable?” She asks us in her cheerful, accented voice.

“Excellent idea, Señora. I’ll help you.” My gaze brushes Anna’s before I exit the room. Our eyes tango together, as she brushes a silky lock of flaxen hair off her face. She’s into me. That’s a good thing, because when this meal is over, she might want to hate me.

Señora Madora appears to be on cloud nine. I need to nip her enthusiasm in the bud before she blurts out one of her ‘predictions’ to Anna.

“Don't say anything to Anna.”

Señora Madora remains her cheerful self. “I know what you’re planning. I have prepared a room for her on the first floor.” She picks up a tray.

“How did you? Never mind.” I pick up the other tray of food. Work was so busy that I hadn’t gotten a chance to ask her.

“You could say ‘thank you’.”

The woman is impossible. It’s probably why I love her so much. She’s also been right in her ‘predictions’ before, and I can’t help but wonder about the one she made about Anna.

“Thank you Señora Madora. Help me out, I don't think she’ll be very happy with me when she realizes that I'm not going to return her home tonight.”

“She won't be happy initially. But you’ll find a way around that.” Señora Madora gives me a mysterious smile.

Chapter 5

Anna

All the wine sipping has left me with a nice buzz, no doubt from an empty stomach. The pair returns carrying two trays laden with food. There are grilled salmon filets, stuffed with rice, baby asparagus coated in butter, a green salad splashed with oil and vinegar, a crusty hunk of French bread, and small bowls of raspberries.

"This looks incredible, Señora Madora. Thank you so much."

"You're quite welcome, Anna." Senora looks pleased.

"Thank you, Senora," adds the Tsar.

She leaves us to our feast, and I dive into the meal with relish. The Tsar is true to his word about Senora being an excellent cook. This is one of the best meals I've ever eaten. He watches me with amusement. "I take it you're not regretting coming here for dinner?"

I laugh, "No regrets at all. I haven't had a meal like this in ages."

"You don't like to cook?"

"I don't know." The wine loosens my tongue, I polish off my glass, and he pours me another. "Thanks." I pause to take a sip, then continue, "I've been fairly busy since college. A friend of mine and I started a coffee shop after graduation. We started small, catering to mostly college kids, doing all the work ourselves in the beginning. It took working all hours and a couple years to break even, but we've finally been able to hire other people so we can have more of a life.

Valentin looks at me with what appears to be admiration. It gives me a warm happy glow inside.

"You're a businesswoman."

"Yes, I didn't want a regular job, answering to a boss and all that. I wanted something different. Plus, I thought if the business did well, I would have time for art. I like to paint, and I'm hoping to be able to buy a fixer upper soon and spend time on that. So, to answer your question, I'm not sure if I like to cook or not. I just haven't had the time for it. I can make a mean southern biscuits and gravy. Other than that, pretty much it's been peanut butter and hot dogs and spaghetti. Cheap and easy."

"And your business partner, he's your boyfriend?" His fingertips align under his jaw, his molten stare making me feel like I could melt into him. There's something magnetic about him, hypnotizing even. He's solidly present and easily the most handsome man I've ever laid eyes on; I can't help but feel attracted to him. The vein in my neck starts to pulse under his scrutiny.

"No. He's one of my best friends, we grew up on the same street. He has a wife and a new baby, that's how I was able to take a leave of absence to come up here. He took six weeks off to help his wife with the baby, and he wanted to offer me the same."

"I'm fortunate that you have chosen this place to take a vacation."

He locks me into his gaze, the warmth of the corners of his eyes betraying a secret mirth that hides behind them. My heart begins to hammer in my chest, as unbidden thoughts of him and me… God, what am I thinking? *Anna get a grip.*

"A woman as beautiful as you, surely must have a lover?"

A shot of heat moves directly under my navel. What a bold question. My heart pounds and my cheeks bloom cherry pink. He's smooth, much smoother than any guy I've ever dated in the South. But he's probably like the rest. Despite the wine, I find that my cynical view of men remains intact. I'm not going to be a convenient one-night stand for this man. I don't care that I have what seems like an animal attraction for him. Or that he looks at me like I'm dessert.

Since Jason, I've remained guarded. Now here I am, two years later, more confident as a woman, but still unsure about the opposite sex. *Damn shame too because you could be missing out on what's right in front of you.* My mind has a way of interjecting these thoughts, but it makes me pause for a second, and realize that I've kind of been stuck in the past, and maybe it's time to move on.

His eyes are like liquid pools drawing me to him.

"I'm single. And incredibly happy about it." Well, maybe that was *a harmless lie*. I was happy, but now that I am experiencing this thing here with him? Whoa. I can't believe what I'm thinking. I better nix the wine sipping.

"I see."

What? He can read my mind? His gaze is intense. Yep, somehow, he knows. The old part of me that hates myself for dating Jason is still here, still feeling shame, even though he is the one that cheated.

I change the subject, "How long have you lived up here? It's such a beautiful place."

"It is beautiful. I'm not considered a 'true Vermonter', but I love it here. I've lived here for about ten years, before this I was in New York City with my family of origin."

"Where is your family now?"

"My parents are deceased, they emigrated from Russia, so my aunts and uncles still live over there. Two of my brothers live on the East Coast, and one moved back to Russia. He lives near my grandmother. I have five nephews, no nieces yet. My wife died young; we had no children." A shadow crosses his face.

"I'm so sorry." We sit in silence for a moment. I feel like I've touched on some sensitive subjects and feel bad for bringing it up, obviously, it's still painful.

Thankfully, Senora appears and breaks the silence. Cheerfully, she asks if we are ready for dessert.

"I am so stuffed," I protest. "And I should be heading home, if you don't mind taking me." I look over at the Tsar.

"Señora Madora, I'll take some please."

Senora leaves, and I stand up. "I don't mean to be rude, but I'm sure the roads are getting slippery, and I don't want you to get stuck out in the storm on my account."

"The roads are slippery, Anna, too much so to head out."

I look at him in disbelief. "I've got to go, you said you would take me back."

"I know what I said, but you would not have come with me otherwise, and I promised the Bennett's I would look after you. Besides, you're hurt."

"I'm not a child that needs looking after," My tone is sharp, as I move towards my coat and hat. "Thank you for your hospitality, but please take me home now." I shoot him a venomous look and make a hobbled break for the door.

"Anna, please. Consider what you're doing. You're putting your life at risk. Señora Madora has prepared a room for you. It even has an extra-large tub for your bathing needs."

"You're unbelievable." A buzzing sensation begins to traverse the length of my spine. He planned this all along, and I've fallen for it.

"I've never been told that, but I take it as a compliment."

Señora Madora enters with a tray of two desserts and coffees and flashes me an apologetic look.

"Thank you, Senora, for a delicious meal. You've triumphed once again."

"You're welcome."

Not wanting to seem like an ingrate, I add my thanks.

The Tsar stands up and moves to the door. "Anna would you like Señora Madora to help you prepare for bed tonight?"

"No, thank you I'm fine, and I would like to go home now."

"Anna, that is impossible with the weather. I'm sorry, but northern Vermont's climate can be harsh. Mother Nature does not always do things our way. Tonight, she is forcing you to stay here with us."

My face flushes. He tricked me.

Señora Madora turns towards me. "Please Anna. Stay. Don't worry about anything. It is safe here. Nothing to worry about. There is a generator if we lose power, and we will take care of you until your ankle is better."

"Thank you Señora Madora, you're very kind."

"My pleasure." She turns towards the Tsar. "Will you be needing anything else Valentin?"

"Not tonight Senora."

"I'm going to retire. Goodnight Anna. I hope you will cook with me and my kitchen sometime."

"Goodnight, Señora Madora. Thank you for everything."

"You're most welcome, Anna." She gives the Tsar a secretive look and walks out of the room carrying the dinner trays.

I begin to head towards the door. Valentin moves more quickly and takes a position directly in front of the door.

"If you're not willing to give me a ride, I'll walk."

"That would not be wise with your injury. Please, see reason Anna."

"I appreciate your concern, but I can take care of myself." I continue to move towards him, expecting him to step aside.

He does not.

"Thank you for having me in your lovely home for dinner."

"My pleasure." His deep-set eyes search mine.

I reach my hand towards him. He meets my handshake with a firm grip but does not move. The corners of his mouth are upturned in a smile, but the edges of his eyes do not crinkle. It is a battle of wills, and I can tell by his expression that he doesn't intend to back down.

"I'm going to go now."

"I'll show you to your room."

"I told you, I'm leaving." By now, any man I've ever met would have given in to my demands, but not this man. "You can't keep me here."

"I can, and I will Anna. You have no experience with these mountains."

“You said you would bring me home. You lied.” My heart thuds in my chest, and a vein in my temple pulses. He isn't like any southern gentleman I’ve ever encountered.

“It was necessary to make you believe that because you were incredibly determined to return to your home. I would have taken you to the Bennett’s earlier, but you refused that offer, and left me with no other choice. Hours have passed, Anna, the snow has piled up. It could be dangerous to drive in.”

“You have 4-wheel drive.”

“You are staying here Anna.”

“Do you have another vehicle I could borrow?”

“I do, but I'm not lending it to you.”

My face glows red hot. “You can't make me stay.” I glare up at him.

“I'm making you stay.”

“And if I walk out of the house?”

“I'll stop you.” He laughs at the expression that arises on my face at his response.

Something akin to stubborn rage rises within me, at being told what to do. But there is no way I can physically overcome him; he’s a sizable man, built like a Mack truck.

“You're at a size disadvantage Anna.”

“I'll call the police on you.”

“Friends of mine but go ahead.” He gestures to the phone. “They will tell you to stay put.”

An alternative plan is already formulating in my mind. I decide to pretend to play his game. “Fine, I'll stay. Lead the way.”

“I am glad you listened to reason Anna. Would you like dessert first?” He offers.

“No, thanks.” My tone is curt.

“As you wish.” The phone rings, and he moves to answer it. “Excuse me one moment Anna.”

Perfect timing. His truck keys are conveniently within my grasp on the end table next to the chair he's been sitting on. With a quick glance at the Tsar, I stealthily nab them and place them in my pocket, while he is preoccupied by the phone. He’s not going to dictate what I can and can't do. I'll wait till he retires for bed, and then I'll take his truck. He has another vehicle. Probably more than one, judging by the size of the garage. It’s huge, just like his massive ego.

Valentin gets off the phone, walks to where I'm seated, and offers his arm. “I thought a room on the ground floor would be acceptable, considering your leg.”

“You're too kind.”

We make our way down the long hall, past elegant wall sconces protruding from stone walls. It reminds me of a medieval Castle, and I’m walking beside my prison guard. We reach the appointed room. He switches the light on for me and shows me the connecting bathroom. He’s right about the tub, it’s wide and deep, and has jets for a Whirlpool bath. If I weren’t so mad right now, I would probably be excited about it.

The room itself is very spacious, the bed canopied, draped in a cream-colored material, and high enough to require a step. The spread matches and appears to be filled with down. At the bottom of the bed is a tufted bench, and on either side of the bed are mahogany nightstands with matching lamps. There is a phone on the stand closest to me.

“Do you need anything, Anna?”

I look up at him. He is more than a full head taller than I am and looks like he either chops wood or frequents the gym, maybe both.

"I'm fine." There's nothing more that I want than to show him that he will not control me, ever. I don't care how sexy he is.

"If you need anything in the night, you can call me or Señora Madora. Dial 1 for me, Senora is 3."

"What room is Senora in?"

"She lives in the guest house."

"Oh."

"I'm sorry that you are disappointed in the outcome of this evening."

"I wouldn't be if you hadn't lied."

"The lesser of two evils."

"You're incredibly arrogant."

He shrugs his shoulders, as if he could care less that I see him for who he really is underneath the strikingly handsome exterior.

"I like a woman with fire." An amused expression crosses his face.

"Do the Bennett's know about you?"

"I told them you would be staying with me. I didn't want them to worry. I believe they felt responsible for you."

"People around here do not need to be responsible for me."

"We are a small community. We look out for each other."

Chapter 6

Anna

He walks out of the room, closing the door behind him. I lean against it, listening to the sound of his footsteps as they retreat down the hall. After 10 minutes pass, I shut the lights out, and open the door with care. There's not a sound. I move slowly, stopping to listen every few steps, wondering where his room is located.

The sound of voices emanates from the sitting room, indicating he's on the phone. Perfect. Ducking down, I creep to the front door, keys clutched to my chest. The double wide door is locked, and it makes a clicking sound, as I cautiously unlatch it. Opening the door slowly, I am unprepared for the gust of wind that meets me. The door leaps out of my hands like a demon in a rage, and slams with a loud 'thunk' into the house.

I know I have only seconds. Racing towards the truck, limping slightly, I trip in my haste, and quickly get back up.

"Anna!" He's behind me now, shouting to me.

Fumbling with the keys, I hit the unlock button for the door, and slip into the driver's seat. It isn't fast enough. The Tsar catches the door as I'm trying to shut it. I struggle against him, trying to remove his arm from the door. "Anna," he says sharply.

"Let me go!" I'm in a blind fury, kicking, and punching at him with all my might.

The keys fall to the passenger side floor. Straining to reach them, I kick at the Tsar with my good foot, trying to keep him out of the truck. Seeing what I'm after, he enters the truck, pinning me beneath him on the leather bench. His arms are longer, and he takes the keys, his body imprisoning mine beneath him. He holds my arms down, as I try desperately to free myself. Finally, I give up for the moment, sweating and panting.

He looks down at me, a ruthless look on his face, "You're a little vixen aren't you? Trying to steal my truck."

"You lied to me."

"A harmless lie for your own safety."

"Get off me."

"Not until you promise to stay here."

"I won't promise."

"Then you will be sleeping in my room, and I'll make sure that you say."

"You can't do that."

"Watch me."

Keeping ahold of my hands, he moves them to a position behind my back and moves our bodies together to a sitting position. I try to fight him with my arms and legs, but he overpowers me. He slides me with him off the seat, holding me tightly. Keeping my arms behind my back, he forces his torso between my legs as his feet hit the ground. I find myself straddling him.

His large hands cover mine, and he moves to push my bottom towards his body into a tight fit, so tight that I can't help but feel his bulging cock press into my belly. Unable to release my hands from his grip, the most movement I can muster is a slight wriggling motion which only serves to send little pulses of pleasure to the juncture of my thighs, as I bump against his erection.

"Let me go." I pant, trying to catch my breath, my body at war between conflicting desires within me. My need to control and my sexual attraction for this beast of a man.

The wind swirls around us, and I taste the cold wetness of the heavily falling snow on the cleft above my top lip, as I lick it away with my tongue. He watches me with amusement, as I stare at him with undisclosed rage. Never in my life have I met someone as ruthless as this man, baring my way from returning to my home away from home. Our breath comes out in cold puffs, mingling together within the heavily falling snow.

He inhales deeply as he watches me, the depths of his eyes searching mine for a connection. He wants me, and it terrifies me. I have never felt an intensity of attraction like this before, maybe because he is a man, and I've only dated boys.

"I'm not staying here." I say with all the coldness I can muster.

His eyes harden. "The time for games is over, Anna."

In one swift motion, he catches me at the waist and swings me over his shoulder like a sack of potatoes, slamming the truck door and making his way to the house through the whirling snow.

"Let me down this instant." I pound at his back and kick my feet. The Tsar appears to be unfazed, wrapping his arms around my legs to ensure that I can no longer kick him.

He carries me inside, my hollering dimmed to the outside world once the thick doors swing shut. We proceed at a fast clip up the grand, circular, wrought iron staircase. Three floors later, we emerge into a spacious suite. He locks the door and throws me down on the King-sized bed.

"Do you realize that people have died here?" He stares down at me ruthlessly. I suppose it is some protective male instinct, but there is something else in those deep dark eyes.

My body goes limp, but my tongue wins out, "You can't hold me here against my will, you're not an actual Tsar, even though you're acting like one."

"I can hold you against your will for your own safety Anna. Think of your family. Would your parents want you alone in a cabin in the middle of nowhere with no electricity and possibly no running water? If the power goes out, the water pipes in your little cabin can freeze. Last time we had a blizzard like this, the roads were not cleared for a week. Not to mention, people have gotten lost wandering from shelter in whiteout conditions and died a few feet from their homes. I already know that you would not listen to me if I told you that you cannot go wandering around outside in conditions like this. Just think of today. What if you had hurt yourself, and I wasn't there?"

My cheeks burn, and I glare at him without speaking for a moment. I hadn't thought of the pipes freezing in the cabin, but I don't want to admit to him that he could be right.

The Tsar, and he really is like a wicked Tsar, I decide, heads over to the door and switches on the lamps that are on either side of the bed. I blink, as my eyes adjust to the light, and survey the suite. Enormous wooden posts spiral to a high ceiling, rising off each corner of the King size bed. There is a bank of skylights across the ceiling and one wall consists of floor to ceiling windows. A sitting area is adjacent to the bedroom, which consists of a marble gas fireplace, above which hangs a wide flat screen TV. A tufted camel colored Ottoman, and a rectangular sectional, along with palm trees in pots make up the rest of the room. Another sitting area is arranged near the bed. Beyond that is a hallway, down which I assume is a bathroom and a closet.

Valentin drags a piece of the sectional over in front of the door. The Ottoman contains thick blankets, and he pulls those out. Next, he comes over to the bed and removes one of the pillows. I move over as he gets near me, and glance at his face. Jaw clenched, his mouth set in a hard line, he gives me a searing glance that speaks volumes. I return the favor.

After setting the pillow and blankets down on his makeshift bed, he gets on the phone that is hanging near the door. "The bathroom is down the hall on the left," he says to me, as he dials. "I'll sleep on the sectional; you can have my bed."

Despite my fury, a tingling sensation shoots from my navel to the juncture of my thighs at the thought of sleeping in his bed. I head down the hall, ears straining to overhear his conversation.

Lights automatically turn on when I enter the bathroom. It's palatial, I've never seen anything like it. There are two sinks with Onyx countertops, the floor tiled in what looks like old world Italian marble. There is a shower to the right with numerous jets, surrounded on two sides by clear glass. On the left is a huge jacuzzi tub with a step to climb up to it and on the far right behind the shower is a toilet and bidet. Palm fans line one shower wall so as to give privacy to the toilets. There are two skylights, and in front of the tub is a picture window that looks down the mountain.

Pausing at the door, I hone in on his phone conversation. "Señora Madora. This is Valentin. Yes, she did agree to say. I just wanted to tell you to stay home tomorrow, I'll cook for Anna and myself. I called Rick, he'll put the word through to the men."

Shutting the door quietly, I place a hand on either side of the sink and release a deep breath, feeling shaky, as my adrenaline wears off. Conflicting feelings war for my attention. Embarrassment, fear, and desire. Embarrassment that Valentin is probably right about me staying in his home. Fear of being alone with him in this huge house. Fear of myself and what we might start together. And desire that I cannot crush away with a simple wish. My thoughts go to the struggle outside, and the feeling of his body pressed into mine. It felt incredibly good, heightened even, with the undercurrent of rage. And I want the feeling back.

Washing my hands and face, I glance in the mirror, and check my appearance. My eyes are glittering strangely, and my hair is an unholy mess. Running shaky fingers through it, I try to straighten the tangles. Unsure of which emotion is going to win out, I eventually emerge and head back down the hall, noticing that the Tsar is sitting at his desk typing on a laptop, and appears to be lost in thought.

Not looking back, I pass him, and walk straight to the door, attempting to push the sectional away, as I pull on the handle. It might take an hour to walk back to the cabin, but I can't stay. Not like this. I'm not going to be forced to be his prisoner.

"Anna, don't do that." His voice is low and dangerous sounding. He's moved very silently behind me, placing his large masculine hand over my smaller feminine one that is currently clutching the nob.

"You can't keep me here Valentin."

"I'm not going to let you leave Anna."

"It's not your choice."

"It is my choice. I choose to keep you here for your own safety."

I look around at him furiously, the anger building. “I won't be kept a prisoner.” I swing towards him, fist raised.

He grabs my wrist and pins it behind my waist along with the other one, prying it off the doorknob. Every struggle I make against him causes him to tighten his grip on me until I can no longer move. Locked within his embrace, I feel the heat of his body against mine.

Valentin looks down at me, his eyes heated with lusty appreciation at the sight of my breasts, exposed and heaving over my shirt from the struggle between us.

The tension between us is palpable. We’ve gone too far, and everything is about to come undone. I glare at him. Part of me wants to hate him, part of me wants him to bring those sensual lips down over mine with enough force to make me forget every negative thing I've ever thought about men.

“I'm going to fuck you.”

My pulse accelerates through the roof at his words, raw and primal. My mind wars within me. I can't do this. Nice girls don't do this.

“And I'm going to make you forget him.” His dark eyes scorch my lighter ones.

END OF EXCERPT

Follow the link to find out what happens next, and thank you for your support!

https://www.amazon.com/dp/B091FSF3L3

www.ingramcontent.com/pod-product-compliance
Lightning Source LLC
LaVergne TN
LVHW052104160826
845678LV00015B/3358
9798847225274